P9-CRE-312

Let's Go, Cubs™!

Aimee Aryal

Illustrated by Miguel De Angel

www.mascotbooks.com

It was a sunny afternoon on Chicago's
North Side. *Cubs* fans from near and far
were on their way to *Wrigley Field* to watch
their beloved Cubs play baseball.

On this day, the Sutter family arrived at the corner of Waveland and Sheffield Avenues ready for an afternoon of baseball. As the family headed to the ballpark, Jimmy Sutter cheered, "Let's go, Cubs!"

Jimmy's sister, Emily, had watched the *Chicago Cubs* play on television many times, but this was her first time at Wrigley Field. Right away, she spotted the famous red marquee outside the ballpark.

Reading the sign, Emily said, "Wrigley Field - Home of the Chicago Cubs." There was a festive mood outside the ballpark. Friendly Cubs fans greeted the Sutter family by cheering, "Let's go, Cubs!"

Mr. Sutter had been going to Cubs games ever
since he was a little boy. His father would bring him
to the ballpark in time for batting practice.

Mr. Sutter was happy to continue this family tradition with his children. Jimmy's favorite player stepped to the plate and hit several balls out of the ballpark. Jimmy cheered, "Let's go, Cubs!"

After batting practice, the family stayed close to the
field and watched the grounds crew prepare the field
for play. One man wheeled away the batting cage.
Another man raked the infield and chalked the lines.

The supervisor of the grounds crew had the honor of inspecting the famous ivy growing on the outfield wall. Satisfied that the field was ready for play, the grounds crew cheered, "Let's go, Cubs!"

Before heading to their seats for the start of the game, there was one more important stop that had to be made - the concession stands! The smell of delicious food was too much to resist!

After grabbing snacks, Emily stopped for a
Cubs pennant, which she waved proudly.
As the Sutter family walked to their seats,
Emily cheered, "Let's go, Cubs!"

As Cubs fans settled into their seats, the public address announcer introduced the Chicago Cubs players. The crowd cheered as each name was announced. The team was dressed in their classic white pinstriped uniforms and blue baseball caps.

It was now time for the National Anthem. The players removed their caps and gazed at the American flag. Beautiful music echoed throughout the ballpark as players and fans sang. Ready to play baseball, the players cheered, "Let's go, Cubs!"

"PLAY BALL!" called the umpire. The Cubs pitcher
walked onto the pitching mound and a batter from
the visiting team stepped to the plate.

The Cubs pitcher delivered a perfect fast
ball. The batter swung with all his might,
but did not connect with the ball.
"STRIKE ONE!" yelled the umpire.

Every seat at Wrigley Field was filled. Some fans even watched the game from the rooftops of nearby buildings! No matter where they were, everyone was enjoying the festive Wrigley Field atmosphere.

As the game continued, a visiting player hit a home run into the left field bleachers. Honoring Wrigley Field tradition, the fan that caught the home run ball threw it back onto the field. Cubs fans seated nearby cheered, "Let's go, Cubs!"

After the visiting team batted in the seventh inning,
it was time for the seventh inning stretch and the
singing of *Take Me Out To The Ballgame*.™

Fans sang arm-in-arm as they enjoyed this Cubs tradition. Some fans had beautiful voices. Some fans did not. But together, the crowd sounded perfect. After the song, everyone cheered "Let's go, Cubs!"

The Cubs trailed by one run with two outs in the bottom of the ninth inning. A Cubs player was on first base as the team's best hitter stepped to the plate. With a powerful swing, the batter launched a deep fly ball over

the left field wall, beyond the left field bleachers,
and onto Waveland Avenue. HOME RUN!
The crowd rose to their feet and cheered,
"Cubs win! Cubs win!"

After the game, the Sutter family celebrated the
Cubs win. All Cubs fans were happy! To mark the
win, a white flag with a "W" flew atop the
center field scoreboard.

The team's great play gave Cubs fans reason to believe that this year would end with a trip to the World Series. Cubs fans everywhere cheered, "Let's go, Cubs!"

For Maya and Anna. ~ Aimee Aryal

For Sue, Ana Milagros, and Angel Miguel. ~ Miguel De Angel

For more information about our products, please visit us online at www.mascotbooks.com.

ISBN: 978-1-932888-84-3
Printed in the United States.
www.mascotbooks.com

MASCOT BOOKS

www.mascotbooks.com

MLB

Boston Red Sox
Hello, Wally!
by Jerry Remy

Wally's Journey Through Red Sox Nation
by Jerry Remy

New York Yankees
Let's Go, Yankees!
by Yogi Berra

New York Mets
Hello, Mr. Met!
by Rusty Staub

St. Louis Cardinals
Hello, Fredbird!
by Ozzie Smith

Chicago Cubs
Let's Go, Cubs!
by Aimee Aryal

Chicago White Sox
Hello, Southpaw!
by Aimee Aryal

Philadelphia Phillies
Hello, Phillie Phanatic!
by Aimee Aryal

Cleveland Indians
Hello, Slider!
by Bob Feller

NBA

Dallas Mavericks
Let's Go, Mavs!
by Mark Cuban

NFL

Dallas Cowboys
How 'Bout Them Cowboys!
by Aimee Aryal

More Coming Soon

Collegiate

Auburn University
War Eagle! by Pat Dye
Hello, Aubie! by Aimee Aryal

Boston College
Hello, Baldwin! by Aimee Aryal

Brigham Young University
Hello, Cosmo!
by Pat and LaVell Edwards

Clemson University
Hello, Tiger! by Aimee Aryal

Duke University
Hello, Blue Devil! by Aimee Aryal

Florida State University
Let's Go 'Noles! by Aimee Aryal

Georgia Tech
Hello, Buzz! by Aimee Aryal

Indiana University
Let's Go Hoosiers! by Aimee Aryal

James Madison University
Hello, Duke Dog! by Aimee Aryal

Kansas State University
Hello, Willie! by Dan Walter

Louisiana State University
Hello, Mike! by Aimee Aryal

Michigan State University
Hello, Sparty! by Aimee Aryal

Mississippi State University
Hello, Bully! by Aimee Aryal

North Carolina State University
Hello, Mr. Wuf! by Aimee Aryal

Penn State University
We Are Penn State by Joe Paterno
Hello, Nittany Lion! by Aimee Aryal

Purdue University
Hello, Purdue Pete! by Aimee Aryal

Rutgers University
Hello, Scarlet Knight! by Aimee Aryal

Syracuse University
Hello, Otto! by Aimee Aryal

Texas A&M
Howdy, Reveille! by Aimee Aryal

UCLA
Hello, Joe Bruin! by Aimee Aryal

University of Alabama
Roll Tide! by Kenny Stabler
Hello, Big Al! by Aimee Aryal

University of Arkansas
Hello, Big Red! By Aimee Aryal

University of Connecticut
Hello, Jonathan! by Aimee Aryal

University of Florida
Hello, Albert! by Aimee Aryal

University of Georgia
How 'Bout Them Dawgs!
by Vince Dooley
Hello, Hairy Dawg! by Aimee Aryal

University of Illinois
Let's Go, Illini! by Aimee Aryal

University of Iowa
Hello, Herky! by Aimee Aryal

University of Kansas
Hello, Big Jay! by Aimee Aryal

University of Kentucky
Hello, Wildcat! by Aimee Aryal

University of Maryland
Hello, Testudo! by Aimee Aryal

University of Michigan
Let's Go, Blue! by Aimee Aryal

University of Minnesota
Hello, Goldy! by Aimee Aryal

University of Mississippi
Hello, Colonel Rebel! by Aimee Aryal

University of Nebraska
Hello, Herbie Husker! by Aimee Aryal

University of North Carolina
Hello, Rameses! by Aimee Aryal

University of Notre Dame
Let's Go Irish! by Aimee Aryal

University of Oklahoma
Let's Go Sooners! by Aimee Aryal

University of South Carolina
Hello, Cocky! by Aimee Aryal

University of Southern California
Hello, Tommy Trojan! by Aimee Aryal

University of Tennessee
Hello, Smokey! by Aimee Aryal

University of Texas
Hello, Hook 'Em! by Aimee Aryal

University of Virginia
Hello, CavMan! by Aimee Aryal

University of Wisconsin
Hello, Bucky! by Aimee Aryal

Virginia Tech
Yea, It's Hokie Game Day!
by Cheryl and Frank Beamer
Hello, Hokie Bird! by Aimee Aryal

Wake Forest University
Hello, Demon Deacon!
by Aimee Aryal

West Virginia University
Hello, Mountaineer! by Aimee Aryal

NHL

Coming Soon

Visit us online at www.mascotbooks.com for a complete list of titles.